TILLY'S PROMISE

TILLY'S PROMISE

Linda Newbery

Barrington Stoke

I KNEW a simple soldier boy

Who grinned at life in empty joy,

Slept soundly through the lonesome dark,

And whistled early with the lark ...

- Siegfried Sassoon

For Yvonne Coppard

First published in 2014 in Great Britain by
Barrington Stoke Ltd
18 Walker Street, Edinburgh, EH3 7LP

www.barringtonstoke.co.uk

ISBN: 978-1-78112-293-8

Printed in China by Leo

Contents

Chapter 1

At War!

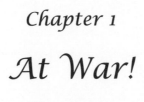

There had been talk and rumours for weeks, but now it was official – we were at war! My father put a notice in our shop window, and people outside stopped to read it.

Our customers talked of nothing else.

"Mr Milton's son's been called back from leave," they would say.

Or, "My Robbie's joining up."

Some were angry about the Germans starting the war. "That Kaiser Bill! Wants to run the whole world, if you ask me."

Others were gloomy and afraid. "The Germans are in Belgium! They'll be over here next, if we don't stop them. It's a short hop across the Channel."

I listened while I fetched things from the shelves and counted coins. I didn't know whether to feel excited or fearful. At war! What did it mean? Would German soldiers march down the street, aiming their rifles at everyone? Would they take over? I shivered. Life in this village was always the same, year after year. In fact, I'd often thought it was too much the same, and wished for a bit more change. But now ...

"That young man of yours will join up, I'm sure!" said Mrs Whitley, while I weighed a pound of sausages.

"Harry?" I felt myself go pink. "Will he?"

"Course!" she said. "All the boys want to do their bit."

I felt a small thrill to hear Harry Brading described as my 'young man' – Harry, with his quick dark eyes, and his shy way of looking at me. We'd always been friends, but of late that had changed. As we walked home from the Bank Holiday fair, he called me his sweetheart. We kissed, but it was quick and clumsy. Then he said he was sorry, as if I might mind. I didn't mind at all! I wanted to try again.

I thought I would feel proud, when I saw Harry in a soldier's uniform. But I didn't want him to go away.

Father closed the shop and cashed up, and I tidied the shelves and swept the floor. It was teatime, and my brother Georgie was home from work.

He was excited, banging his knife on the table. "War! I want to go to the war!" he told us.

"No, Georgie, no," Mother soothed. "You can't go. You're not old enough – thank goodness. And you've got your job. You like your job."

"Want to go." Georgie pretended to aim a rifle. "Fight. Kill some Germans!"

"You don't want to kill anyone," Father told him. "War isn't fun and games."

I spread honey on bread for him – he got into a sticky mess if he did it himself. "There you are, Georgie," I said. "Fruit bread, your favourite."

It was like having a much younger brother, even though Georgie was 16 now and taller than me. He was a big, strong boy, but he'd always been slow to learn. My parents had worried about what he'd do when he left school.

For a while he helped in the shop, where he only made muddles, and extra work.

Then Mr Milton offered Georgie a job at Brockbank Hall, working in the gardens. That solved the problem very well. Albert, the head gardener there, understood Georgie. He was kind to him and gave him simple jobs to do. Georgie loved to groom and feed Bramble, the fat pony who pulled the mowing-machine. He'd have spent all his time in the stables if he could, but the Miltons' other horses were too valuable, and needed expert handling. Still, Georgie loved Bramble and saw him every day, and was happy.

As the hot days of August went by, more and more of the village boys joined the Essex Regiment – those who were old enough, anyway. Harry was one of them. He and two friends went to sign up at the army barracks.

"I don't want to leave you, Tilly Peacock," he told me. "But I can't stay at home and pretend nothing's happening."

"I know you can't! *I'd* go, if I were a boy."

We stood by the churchyard wall and looked out at the fields. The trees threw long shadows, and pigeons cooed in the elms.

"Now you'll have the chance to cross the Channel," I said. In a way I wished I could go, too. Harry and I often talked of the countries we'd like to visit – China, India, Australia ... Oh, there was the whole world! It was a game we played.

"I'll come back," Harry promised. "And – will you wait for me, Tilly Peacock?"

"Of course I will."

"It won't be for long," Harry said. "They say we'll have the Germans beaten by Christmas. I'll write to you – and will you write back?"

6

"You know I will!"

The kissing was a little better this time. Our arms tightened round each other. We only broke apart when old Mr Brownlee tramped along the path, calling for his dog.

Chapter 2

Nurse Tilly

Harry was sent to an army camp near Colchester, where he'd spend the next few months in training. Before he left, he said that he'd think of me in the shop every day, exactly as usual. But soon I had other plans.

Part of Brockbank Hall was turned into a hospital and I heard that volunteer nurses were needed. I wanted to help.

"I could learn to be a nurse!" I told my parents. "Just because I'm a girl, it doesn't mean I can't be useful."

My mother said, "How will you like it, though? There'll be blood. And wounds. And worse." And my father said that he needed me in the shop.

It took me a few days to get my own way. Mary Abbot, the blacksmith's daughter, had left school and was looking for work. That gave me an idea. Mary could take my place in the shop and I'd go to Brockbank Hall. Mary was a steady, sensible girl, and my father had to agree.

"As for the blood and the wounds," I told my mother, "I'll have to get used to it. I'd be no use if I screamed and ran away, would I?"

When I reported for duty I had second thoughts. How could I be a nurse when I knew nothing?

At least I *looked* like a nurse in my uniform of a dress, apron and cuffs. And the patients called me 'Nurse', as if I'd been doing it for years.

The work wasn't difficult and soon I felt disappointed. For the most part I just rolled bandages and served tea and meals.

It felt odd to be in such a grand house. The long drawing room of Brockbank Hall had been cleared of furniture and two rows of beds brought in. As the men lay in bed, they could look up at the fancy plaster on the ceiling, painted with angels and cherubs. Tall windows gave views of the lawn sweeping down to the lake.

Sometimes I saw Georgie outside as he swept up leaves, or led Bramble over the grass. Bramble lived alone in the stable and the paddock now, as the army had taken the bigger horses. Mr Milton's younger son James had joined up, and his brother Charles was already a captain.

Some of the patients were young men. Others were my father's age, or older. Most weren't very ill – they had been sent here to build up their strength after being in hospital in London. On warm days, those who could walk went out to look at the gardens or to sit under the trees, where they talked or read.

My eyes filled with tears when I saw a young soldier lurching down the path on crutches. He was no older than Harry. One of his trouser legs was pinned back at the knee – his foot and lower leg had been amputated. Imagine getting used to that! What if it happened to Harry? Others had bandaged heads, arms in slings – one man had lost an eye.

"Tears are no use," the ward sister said on my first day. "You must act as if all this is normal. Always be bright and brisk. That's your job."

I tried. I was astonished how cheerful some of the men were, too, in spite of their wounds.

One afternoon I was pushing a sergeant out to the terrace in his wheelchair. The one-legged soldier, Frank, was crossing the lawn, quite fast now on his crutches. Georgie was plodding up from the orchard with a basket of apples.

When Georgie saw how Frank hopped and swung over the grass, he laughed and pointed. He copied him, spilling apples as he lurched.

"What are you looking at?" Frank shouted. "Turnip-head!" He dangled his arms loose over his crutches, like an ape, and let his mouth hang open.

"Georgie, stop it!" I left the sergeant and ran down the lawn. "Pick up those apples and get along to the kitchen." Then I turned on Frank. "You mustn't make fun of him like that! It's unkind. He's my brother."

"Oh, sorry, Nurse Tilly." At once Frank was shame-faced. "It's just –" He looked down at his missing leg.

"I know." I touched his arm. "Georgie was only interested. It's all new to him. He didn't mean anything."

I felt angry with both of them. Sorry for both of them, too.

It had been like this at school – other boys made silly faces and copied the way Georgie spoke. They called him 'Monkey Brain', 'Dunce', 'Blockhead'. Sometimes Georgie provoked them, sometimes not.

I tried to forget about it, and went back to the sergeant in his wheelchair on the terrace. Soon Frank came over on his crutches and laughed and joked with the sergeant in the sunshine. Frank caught my eye with a look that said, 'Sorry. I won't do it again.'

That evening, at home, I tried to explain to Georgie.

"You must never point, or laugh, when you see people with arms or legs missing, or bandaged heads," I told him. "It's awful for them. Imagine if it was you!"

Georgie pushed out his bottom lip and looked down. He knew he'd done something wrong even if he didn't understand why.

I knew it wouldn't be the last time. Georgie couldn't stop staring at the wounded men because they'd been to war. He'd been told to do his work and not bother them, but often he went up to them in the garden. He wanted to know about shells and guns, and what the Germans looked like.

The men didn't have much to do and most of them were happy to chat to Georgie. But if he laughed at their wounds or their missing limbs, who could blame them for being sharp?

There was no sign of the fighting being over by Christmas.

Harry wrote every week. At New Year he came home from camp to spend a few days with his family. He was a lance corporal now, and he wore a stripe on his sleeve to show his new rank. He gave me a bracelet for a present, and I'd knitted him a scarf. We sang carols in the church and went for walks together.

All too soon, Harry returned to camp to finish his training. In March he was sent out to France.

Chapter 3

White Feather

As the seasons changed, it became hard to remember what life was like before the war.

Mr Milton's elder son, Charles, was wounded by a bomb blast and would never walk again. Mrs Pickett's son Robbie was Missing in Action.

Everyone dreaded the sight of the Post Office boy on his bike in case he had a telegram with bad news.

It was rare now to see a young man in ordinary clothes rather than in uniform. Mother took Georgie into town on his free afternoon to buy new boots, and came back in a fury.

The first I knew was when I got home and Georgie waved a white feather in my face.

"Where did you get that, Georgie?" I asked.

"Someone gave it to him in town," Mother said. "A cheeky young madam."

I knew what it meant. People gave white feathers to men who weren't soldiers or sailors to tell them they were cowards. Shirkers.

"What happened?" I asked Mother.

"I was talking to Mrs Pickett, with my back turned, or I'd have given that girl a piece of my mind," Mother said. "Georgie – well, he was pleased. He likes feathers. He wouldn't let me take it away. He carried it all afternoon, even though people stared."

"It doesn't matter," I told her. "It didn't mean anything to him."

It was my last week at home. At Brockbank Hall I'd moved on from tea and bandages long ago – now I was dressing wounds and caring for the really ill patients. Next week I was going to a big London hospital. I might even apply to go to France. I wanted to be where nurses were most needed. Maybe in France I'd be able to meet Harry.

By now everyone was talking about conscription. All single young men would be called up to join the army, whether they wanted to or not. Mother was worried about Georgie, who'd soon be 18.

I tried to comfort her. "Georgie can't go!"

"All young men of fighting age must go," she said. "That's what they say."

"He won't pass the tests," I said. "We needn't worry."

In London I shared a bedroom in the nurses' hostel with Dorothy, a girl from Devon. We worked long hours, often all night. Wounded soldiers arrived from France and Belgium in an endless stream, brought up from the Channel ports by train. Many were on stretchers, pale and groaning, or close to death.

How many more could there be? Sometimes I thought there must be no men left to fight.

On my first shift, a boy died just before dawn – a sweet-faced boy no older than me. He'd been gassed so badly that his lungs would never recover, and there was no hope. I was with him as his last painful breath juddered out of him. At last his suffering was over.

For the rest of that day I felt blank with shock. But death was part of the routine. As soon as a patient died, the body was taken away and the bed was stripped and re-made. Within an hour, someone else would be lying there.

Often I was worn out by the time I got to bed, and my dreams were full of the things I'd seen.

The good days were when a letter came from Harry. He wasn't allowed to say where he was, but I understood that he'd be moving up to the front line very soon.

I longed to see him, but I dreaded that one day he'd end up here in the hospital – gassed, or missing a leg, or an eye, or wounded too badly to be saved.

When a telegram arrived from home, I dreaded bad news about Harry.

But the news was of Georgie. His call-up papers had arrived. He was to report to the barracks.

I took the train home as soon as I had a free afternoon.

"It must be a mistake," I told my parents. "How can Georgie be a soldier?"

"There's nothing wrong with his body," my mother said. "They'll pass him as fit for service."

"We're going to appeal," said my father. "That's our only chance. I wish we'd found him a farm job! Farm workers don't have to go."

Mother sighed. "It's all right for Mr Dobson at Vale Farm. Three strapping sons, all at home."

I tried to make the best of it. "Perhaps it won't be too bad. He might work in the kitchens – or even look after the horses. He could do that. He'd like it."

The army rejected my parents' appeal. Georgie went to training camp, full of pride at the idea of being a soldier.

I wrote to Harry with the news. When he replied, he said he had a week's leave at the end of June and hoped to see me.

We made plans. But at the last moment Harry's leave was called off.

There was talk of a Big Push over in France. At the hospital that would mean large numbers of wounded men. Anyone fit to be moved was sent on to smaller hospitals to recover. Beds were made up ready for the new patients.

It felt strange to look at the rows of empty beds. I hated to think of the men and boys over in France who'd soon be here, groaning and sweating and dying. But this Push would win the war, people were saying.

When the shelling started, it was so loud that the boom of the big guns in France could be heard in London. It was the start of the attack – intended to wipe out the German trenches before our troops advanced. It was dreadful to think of human beings facing such terror, hour after hour – even Germans. Dorothy and I tried to sleep because we knew we'd work hard in the days to come. But we lay awake for most of the night.

"The German trenches must be smashed to bits. Serves them right," said Dorothy. "They started it."

Next day, the newspaper headlines said 'GREAT BRITISH ATTACK BEGINS'.

Would it really be the beginning of the end?

The waiting was soon over. All day and all night wounded men arrived at Charing Cross station and were brought to us by ambulance. Some of them made the painful journey to London only to die as they reached the ward.

Every time I peeled off blood-soaked bandages or filthy clothing I feared what I'd find underneath. There were cuts and gashes and bullet wounds, dressed in a rush. Dirty wounds could turn septic, or the flesh could rot and die. All of us nurses, and the doctors, rushed to and fro, doing what we could. It was never enough. Beds and mattresses were crammed into every spare space, and even the huts outside were turned into wards.

What sort of victory could cost so many lives?

The men – those who could speak – weren't talking of victory. They were talking of a bloodbath.

The shells had failed to cut the German wire. The Germans had deep, safe trenches. When the shelling stopped, they were ready. Our soldiers had walked into terrible machine-gun fire.

"And we're the lucky ones," a sergeant said. "We're still here." He talked of bodies caught on the German wire. He spoke of the screams of wounded and dying men, of running wildly in a rush of terror.

"It was hell," said the man in the next bed, eyes closed.

After hours of this, I was too tired to think clearly. At last the sister told me to go and get something to eat and drink.

I struggled to swallow. My mind was full of what machine-gun bullets could do to human flesh. My nose was full of the reek of blood and mud, pus and sweat and carbolic soap.

And beneath all that, I felt a nagging pain of worry.

Where was Harry?

Chapter 4

Promises Made

At last, a letter came. It was from France and had taken two weeks to arrive.

The letter was short. Harry said that he'd been in the attack and had been in hospital in France with a minor head wound. (I hoped he wasn't making light of something serious.) Now he was going home on leave to recover. He asked if I could get time off, and go home to the village too.

The Sister said that was out of the question. I could take an afternoon off, no more. We'd

have to make do with a meeting in London
before Harry took the train out to Essex.

I counted the days. Nothing must get in the
way!

Georgie didn't write letters, but sometimes
he sent a postcard with just his name on it
and the address in clumsy writing. I knew this
from my mother's weekly letters.

'He's going out to France at the end of the
month,' my mother wrote. 'I hoped the war
would end before he got that far, but no one's
talking about the end any more, are they? At
least he's in A Company, the same as Harry.'

This was good. Harry could send me news
of Georgie.

But the next letter from home was a sad
one. Mr Milton's younger son, James, was
dead – killed in the first of the fighting. He'd
been an officer in A Company, a good one,
and well liked, as I knew from Harry's letters.

I was sad for James, who had often called "Good Morning" to me as he rode past on his horse. Sad for Mr Milton, too. Now one son was an invalid, the other dead.

The weather had turned hot and we sweltered in the wards. At the end of my shift on the day I was to meet Harry, I went to my room to tidy myself up. In the bathroom mirror, I looked at my tired eyes and my lank hair. My hands were rough and sore from being washed in disinfectant. I *smelled* of disinfectant, too. What would Harry think?

But when we met outside the hostel, Harry only smiled as if he saw nothing wrong.

"I've been thinking of you every single day, Tilly Peacock. And here you are, just as pretty as I remember. No, prettier."

"Oh, don't be silly!" I couldn't help laughing. "I've been thinking of you, too. And worrying. How *are* you?"

I could see a bandage under his cap. His face was thinner and more serious than I remembered.

"I'm fine," he said. "You're working too hard, though. I can tell."

"But it's nothing compared to what you've been doing, Harry. What the men say – it sounds terrible, the fighting."

"Well, it was. Is." Harry looked bleak. "You heard about James Milton?"

"Yes, from Mother. What happened?"

Harry was silent for a moment. Then he said, "It was awful." His voice was unsteady. "We were in a trench, waiting to go. That was the longest few seconds of my life. He – James – was to lead us. He was brave, trying to keep our spirits up. 'Stay steady,' he said, 'and follow orders.' I was next to him while we waited. And in the last moment, Tilly, before he blew his whistle, I saw his face and

32

I knew he was as scared as I was. Scared of letting himself down. Scared of letting *us* down. Then –" Harry closed his eyes. "The whistle. Over we went. And it was madness. We'd been told to walk, not run, but everyone was running, into a hail of fire and yelling and falling and trying to carry on. James went down right in front of me. He didn't make a sound. I saw his face, and the front of his tunic all torn and bloody, and I knew he was a goner."

"Oh, Harry." I didn't know what else to say.

"He was a good officer," Harry said. "Always kind to the men."

"And – what happened to you?"

"I ran on. I thought my turn would be next, any minute. Then a shell exploded quite close and next thing I was flying through the air. That's all I remember."

I shivered as I thought of it. "You could easily have been killed too."

"Several times over. Maybe I'm not really here. Maybe this is a dream."

"Well, I'm sure *I'm* here," I told him. "And you seem real enough to me."

"I didn't do anything, though, did I?" Harry said. "Nothing brave, nothing of any use at all. I just got hit by a bit of shrapnel, then took up a hospital bed for a few days."

"It wasn't your fault!" I said. "How could it be? What could anyone do?"

Harry put an arm round me. "Let's not talk about it any more."

In the park there were women with prams, and small children. A nanny pointed at the ducks and a bold white one waddled close and tugged at her skirt. But you couldn't get away from the war. There were wounded soldiers in

their dark blue uniforms, and off-duty nurses like me. A group of army officers strolled by the lake, smoking and chatting.

Arm in arm, Harry and I headed for the shade of the trees. Matron was very strict about nurses in uniform meeting their sweethearts and another girl had been in trouble for it last week, but I didn't care. I wanted to cling to every moment. We had such a short time.

"What will you do at home?" I asked.

"Go to Brockbank Hall to see Mr Milton. The captain's written a letter about James – I'll take that to him. And I'll visit my aunt and uncle, and help Pa in the garden. It'll be strange, Tilly. They've got no idea – I know from their letters. They go on about me being a hero, part of a great victory. It's not like that."

I thought of the men in the ward, the ones who shouted out in their sleep as they relived the terror in their dreams.

"Even this." Harry touched the edge of bandage above his ear. "They'll think it's a badge of honour. I won't be able to tell them how it was. Even if I could, it wouldn't be fair."

"After it's over, perhaps," I said. "When you're ..." I hardly dared say it. "... safe."

"You know, it's hard to think of 'after'," Harry said. "Perhaps there won't be any after."

I gripped his arm. "Don't say that!"

"But you know, in a strange way, I want to be back over there," he said. "It doesn't feel right, not being with the others."

I was silent, a little hurt, because Harry seemed to be saying that it didn't feel right to be with me.

Then he laughed. "Except that being with you feels like the rightest thing of all. I'm lucky, Tilly."

"And I'm lucky too."

Harry turned to face me. "You'll wait for me, won't you, Tilly Peacock?"

He'd said this before, in the churchyard at home. This time he sounded more serious – as if it mattered more than anything.

"You know I will!" I told him, serious too. "You don't need to ask. Even if the war goes on forever, I'll still wait for you."

"You promise?" he said quietly.

"Of course."

"I love you, Tilly Peacock."

"Do you mean that?" I felt a little giddy.

"I never say anything I don't mean," he said.

I think I already knew that.

"I love you, Harry Brading," I told him.

It felt dangerous, saying those words –
flying too high, wanting too much. But
wonderful, too. After a few moments we
walked on, with slow steps, as if slowness
would make our time together last longer.

"Will you promise me something, too?"
I asked.

"Anything."

"It's about Georgie." I stopped again. "He's
going out to France, any day now. He'll be in
A Company, same as you. That's good, isn't it?"

"Is it?"

"Maybe he'll even be in your platoon. Will
you look after him?"

Harry looked away, out over the lake.
"Well ... I don't know."

I felt the small niggle of a new hurt. Harry wasn't pleased that Georgie would be in A Company. Perhaps he'd be ashamed to admit that he knew Georgie from home. That didn't seem like the Harry I knew, the Harry I loved.

I tried again. "Oh, please, Harry! It'd be such a comfort to my parents, to know you're keeping an eye on Georgie. You will, won't you? Promise?"

Harry looked away again, and gave a small sigh. "Yes, Tilly, I will. I promise."

"Oh, thank you!"

He held me close and I hugged him back. I felt mean for my unkind thoughts. I was due back on the ward soon, and Harry would head for Liverpool Street Station and his train home. But now the sun was shining and pigeons were crooning in the trees, and all was well.

Chapter 5

Out to France

Dorothy and I had both applied to go to France. Late in the autumn, our orders arrived. We were to go to Boulogne, and on by railway to the base hospital at Étaples, along the coast.

I was excited at the thought of crossing the Channel. I'd seen the sea only a few times. The work would be as hard as in London, but we'd have some time off to explore. Maybe we'd even learn to speak French! And I'd be in the same country as Harry, maybe not all that far apart. There might be chances to meet.

I wrote with my news and Harry replied that he'd come to see me if there was any way he could. He'd moved up towards the border with Belgium – a mining area, he wrote, with coal-heaps and industry. It was very different from the chalk uplands where they'd been fighting in July. Georgie was in a different platoon, but Harry saw him often and he seemed happy. They were at a camp behind the lines, and Georgie spent his spare time with the horses, grooming and talking to them.

⁑⁑

The sea was grey and wind-tossed as the ship pulled out into the Channel. The deck was packed with soldiers looking back at the cliffs. Mist clung to my clothes and eyelashes. In the haze, the famous cliffs of Dover were grey rather than white. Many of the soldiers on

board must be wondering if this would be their last sight of England.

As we stepped ashore at Boulogne, I told myself, 'You're in France, really in France!' But France was fighting to survive against the German invaders. I felt a thrill of strangeness and danger. I was in the same country as the enemy.

The hospital at Étaples looked like a camp – rows of wooden huts and tents, away from the town. It was in a flat area of sand and dunes close to a river mouth. I could smell the sea, taste salt on my lips.

Dorothy and I unpacked our things in the tent we were to share. What would it be like here in the worst of winter?

The matron greeted us and asked about our nursing in London. We were to start work at once, in different wards.

The wards were bigger tents, lined with beds. Canvas was spread over the floor. There was a tremble in the air, which I realised was the heavy guns on the front line. I was closer to the fighting than ever before.

And another thing was very different – the patients in this ward were German.

I was upset about this. I hadn't come to France to nurse Germans! They were the enemy – Jerry, the Hun. At home, since the start of the war, there had been awful stories. People said that the Germans nailed prisoners to crosses, stabbed babies with pitchforks and cut off people's hands. I thought of them as big hard men, full of bloodlust, fearsome in their strange helmets that looked like coal-scuttles.

But I'd never heard any of these things from the soldiers in the other hospitals, or from Harry.

"Get on with it," said the sister, who'd told me to empty the bedpans. "There's no time to stand and gawp. Yes, they're Huns. Yes, they've been trying to kill our boys. Someone still needs to look after them."

The patients in the ward looked exactly like those I'd seen in London – older men, younger men, some who looked too young to be here at all. There were the same wounds – eyes covered with bandages, missing limbs, shrapnel gashes.

I got down to work.

Most of the Germans didn't speak English, so I soon learned to use hand-signals, nods and smiles. Some of the men smiled back, and more than one said, "*Danke, Schwester.*" They thought I was a sister!

These men were prisoners, as well as patients. Several were dying, but those who survived would be sent to England as soon as

they were well enough, and would stay there till the war ended. A few were bitter and angry, but others seemed glad to be out of the fighting.

It was strange to care for men from the other side. I couldn't help thinking that one of them might have killed James Milton or fired the shell that wounded Harry. But soon I stopped thinking of them as 'the enemy'. They were victims of war, like the others I'd seen. They didn't hate the British soldiers.

The first Christmas of the war, people said that British and German soldiers met in No Man's Land to swap cigarettes and kind words. Next day they went back to shooting at each other.

Was that madness, or was it hopeful? I couldn't decide. It seemed that the war itself was the enemy and the men on both sides must struggle to survive. The war was a hungry monster, always wanting more.

After a while I picked up a few words of German. There were two Germans who helped with routine jobs on the ward. Both spoke a little English, which was a help as they could interpret and explain.

Some of the patients could speak a little English too. One of them was a young man from Bonn who'd visited England before the war. His eyes were bandaged and he had other injuries as well.

"There are good eye hospitals in London," I told him, but he looked sad and said, "No good for me. I will not leave here, I think."

His name was Karl and he was 21. He had a sweetheart at home. "On my last leave," he told me, "I ask her to marry me, and she says yes. I will show her to you." He tried to sit up, but the effort was too much. "In my kit-bag," he said. "A photograph."

I looked in the bag under his bed. From the front pocket I took a photograph of a lovely, laughing girl. "She's very pretty!" I told him.

Karl held out his hand and I gave him the picture even though he couldn't see it.

"Yes, I think, very much," he said. "Her name is Maria. Your voice reminds me of her, *Schwester* Tilly. You have a sweetheart, perhaps?"

"Yes." I felt the usual tremor of fear in case it was bad luck to say so. "Harry. He's at the front, near the Belgian border."

"That's where I was too." Karl lay back, worn out. "I wish you good luck, you and your Harry."

Next time I came on duty, the sister told me that Karl was dying.

"He won't last the night," she said. "He's bleeding inside. The doctors can't do anything."

I think I must have known, but still I was shocked.

I went to Karl's bed.

"Karl, it's me," I said. "Tilly."

He reached out a hand. "Not much long," he said. His voice was weak. "*Schwester* Tilly – be with me at the end. Please. Will you promise?"

"I promise," I whispered.

It would be difficult with so many patients to attend to. But I'd keep watching, keep coming back to his bed every few minutes – for as long as he was here.

Chapter 6

A Promise Broken

A long string of lorries arrived in the night with dozens of seriously wounded patients. Many needed emergency operations. We were already full, but now stretchers were laid on the floor in every spare space. It was even worse in the next ward where the worst cases had been taken.

"Tilly, they need you through there," Sister told me. "I'll manage here."

"But I can't!" I looked over at Karl, who was sleeping.

"I'll watch him," she said. "Now go."

"Could you call me if –?" I began, but I knew it was hopeless to ask. There was no time to sit with someone who was quietly dying and couldn't be saved.

I could have wept with tiredness and pity. But there was no time to do anything but help where I was needed. Some of the soldiers arriving now had terrible wounds. The worst were given morphine to ease their pain, but nothing more could be done. In the tiny theatre, operations went on all through the night.

When I came back to my own ward, Karl lay dead.

"He's gone," Sister said. "At least it was peaceful. Not like some of those poor souls."

"Oh ..."

The bed was needed. Helpers carried Karl's body away.

It was too much. Sister's face blurred as I went giddy and swayed on my feet. I couldn't go on – I couldn't! I wanted to sink to the ground and lie there.

"You're worn out," said Sister. "Go and get some sleep. Our shift finished over an hour ago."

"But I promised!" I whispered. "I promised to be with him at the end!"

"Well, you *shouldn't* have promised," she said. "You can't promise anything in all this. You did what you could. Now, look after yourself. Go on! Off you go for some food and a good sleep."

I found my way back to the tent in a haze of tears. I thought of Karl, so brave in the face of death. I'd promised to be with him, but had let him down. I couldn't bear to think of that. Nor of pretty Maria, at home in Bonn – waiting, and not knowing.

After that I was ill for nearly a week and could only leave my bed to visit the toilet and bath-hut. Dorothy came with hot drinks and did everything she could to look after me.

When I was fit for work, I was moved to a ward with less terrible cases, British ones this time. Dorothy and I spent our time off duty together. We walked among the sand dunes and looked out to sea, and explored the busy town of Étaples. It was a fishing-port, crowded now with soldiers coming and going from the training camps nearby.

The huts and tents were bitterly cold in the winter, exposed to wind and gusts of rain. Another Christmas came, another New Year.

Harry wrote at least once a week. We made plans, hoping we could both get leave at the same time. It seemed an age since our meeting in London.

Sometimes I thought I'd forgotten the sound of his voice. I remembered nearly everything

he'd said, but couldn't *hear* him. I had a photograph and I looked at it every night as I got into bed. Whenever a letter came, I was dizzy with relief – it meant he was alive. But really it only meant he'd been alive when he wrote it, a few days or a week ago. Anything could have happened since then, and I could be like poor Karl's Maria, clinging to useless hope.

Harry wrote about endless journeys by train and by lorry, of long days marching, of nights in farm buildings. Now A Company was behind the lines, soon to move up to the front. Georgie was well, Harry said, apart from a few blisters on his feet.

The post also brought a card from Georgie, with a black-and-white picture of a town called Béthune. Georgie had only scribbled his name, and the hospital address was in Harry's writing. That made it special – Georgie's and Harry's writing on the same card. I liked to think of Harry helping Georgie, looking after him.

Chapter 7

Telegram

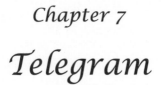

When a telegram arrived, I felt too sick to open it at first. It could only be bad news.

It was from my parents.

'Dreadful news. Georgie killed in action. Will write.'

The words jumbled into nonsense. I stared and stared, willing them to say something different.

This wasn't a dream. Wasn't a nightmare. It was real.

Dover's white cliffs were brilliant in sunshine as the ship pulled into the harbour. Gulls wheeled above the deck, against a clear blue sky. When I had sailed to France, the cry of the gulls had seemed exciting to me. Now their cries sounded like wailing.

This wasn't the return I'd looked forward to. I longed to see my parents, but the house would be empty of Georgie.

Life would never be the same again. My life had already changed in ways I'd never expected. Now this.

Georgie was only one of several from the village who'd died. Three others from his class at school had been killed in the Big Push last summer. But that didn't make the loss any easier.

At home, I was reminded of Georgie everywhere I looked. His place at the table. His bedroom, with the horse picture above the bed. His gardening boots by the back door, his cap on the peg. The postcards he'd sent, propped on the shelf above the fire.

I cried in the kitchen with my mother. Father was busy in the shop, but when he came in for tea there were more tears. No one felt much like eating.

"We had this from Captain Perry." My mother showed me a letter. "And one from Harry. But I expect he wrote to you too."

"No!" I said. "But he'd have sent it to the hospital. It'll be waiting there."

The captain's letter was short. He said how sorry he was for our loss and that Georgie had been a good soldier, always reliable. There

wasn't much about Georgie's death – only
that he was shot by a sniper and was killed
instantly. Captain Perry hoped we'd take
comfort from the fact that Georgie had died for
his King and Country.

"I suppose he has to write lots of letters
like that." I was disappointed. The letter could
have been about anyone.

I expected more from Harry.

His letter said:

Dear Mr and Mrs Peacock,

You will have had the awful news about
Georgie. I am so very sorry for your loss.

I know that Captain Perry has written to
you with the details. There is not much

to add, as I did not see what happened.
But I wanted to tell you that Georgie
had some happy times while he was in
A Company. He seemed cheerful and I
often heard him whistling, just like he did
at home.

I was able to attend his funeral and pay
my last respects to a friend I have known
all my life.

Nothing I write can make up for your
loss, but I wish you all well and hope
these few words will bring some small
comfort.

Yours sincerely,
Harry Brading

I stroked Harry's name with my finger, then put the letter on the table and kept looking at it.

"Wasn't that kind?" my mother sniffed. "He's a good boy, your Harry."

"Yes, it was kind." But again I felt disappointed. I'd wanted Harry to tell us more – how Georgie had been hit, and what he'd been doing. Perhaps it was true that Harry didn't know.

But also I knew that 'killed instantly' were often just words the army used to save relatives from knowing that their son, brother or husband had died a horrible death. Was Harry hiding something?

And he hadn't said anything about *me* in the letter, not once.

That evening I spent a long time writing to him.

When I woke next morning I thought for a moment that I heard Georgie whistling.

I raised my head from the pillow. No, of course it wasn't – only a bird in the tree outside.

I'd never hear Georgie again.

Chapter 8

No Reply

My leave was soon over and I made the long journey back to Étaples.

I was eager for Harry's letter, or letters – most likely there'd be more than one.

There was only a postcard with a single word beside the address. 'Sorry.'

'He must have sent that in a hurry, with a letter to follow,' I thought. But there was nothing more.

I asked Dorothy, I checked the mail rack, and I searched all over in case my precious letter had fallen to the ground or been kicked to one side.

Something had happened to Harry after he sent the postcard. It was the only way to explain his silence.

My mind raced with awful things that might have happened.

No. No. I couldn't bear it, after losing Georgie!

I was due on the ward, but when my shift was over I wrote home. I told my parents I was back safe and asked for any news – even bad news.

A few days later, a reply came. My mother wrote that they were short of everything in the shop – no jam, marmalade or sugar for the customers. I didn't care about jam and sugar! In haste I scanned the pages to see if she'd said anything about Harry.

Yes! Mother had seen Harry's mother at church. Harry had written from Béthune – he was a good boy, Mrs Brading said. He wrote every week. Never missed.

In that case, I thought, *my* letter must have got lost. It was frustrating, but others would come soon.

I wrote to Harry again, to tell him that I loved and missed him. I thanked him for his letter to my parents and for his kind words about Georgie. I told him how his letter to me had gone missing and how sorry I was not to have it, and how much I'd look forward to his next one.

Days passed, then weeks. No reply.

By now the only news of Harry came from my parents, who got it from his mother. He'd been in the front line again. The new officer who had replaced James Milton had been badly hurt. The one sent in *his* place wasn't nearly so good to the men.

I read my mother's letters with growing despair. There was only one thing that could explain this now – and I didn't want to think of it.

Harry had changed. He didn't love me any more. Didn't even care enough to send me a short note.

In November my mother wrote to say that Harry had been home on leave. He'd visited them and they'd shared memories of Georgie. 'So kind of him,' my mother wrote. 'He asked after you. Such a shame you couldn't get leave. When will you see each other?'

So he hadn't told them it was over. Why not? Wouldn't that be fairer to everyone?

I felt hurt and confused. I didn't know what to do, except throw myself into work and try to forget.

It was impossible. Every time an ambulance came in I wondered if Harry might

be on one of the stretchers. What would happen then? Would he speak to me? Once, I thought I saw him propped in one of the beds. I felt myself trembling. Then the young man turned his head and he didn't look much like Harry after all.

I told Dorothy.

"Has he met someone else?" I said. "Could that be it? In London, perhaps? Or a French girl, in Béthune?"

"I don't suppose so," Dorothy soothed. "I expect he's been too busy, that's all."

It was a feeble excuse and we both knew it. Too busy to send even a short note? But he'd said he loved me. And he'd told me that he never said anything he didn't mean.

Well, he didn't love me *now*. Didn't want me.

It was the only thing that made any sense.

69

Chapter 9

Under Fire

The graveyard was spreading down to the sea. Rows of wooden crosses reached ever further. Each day there were new heaps of sandy soil, new graves.

Dorothy and I went out on mild days to walk over the dunes to the beach, but the graves were a sad reminder of all that had been lost.

How much longer could it go on? Stream after stream of new soldiers arrived at the camps, soon to join the hundreds buried here. And this was only one hospital, one graveyard.

A small funeral party was in the graveyard now. A bugler played 'The Last Post', and the final note trembled on the breeze.

"Sometimes I think there are more dead than alive," Dorothy said.

I shivered. "I know. No soldiers left, only ghosts."

When December turned to January, people didn't speak of 'Victory this year', the way they used to. Everyone was too worried that the war would end in defeat, not victory.

The soldiers who arrived in the wards brought us frightening news. They'd been so outnumbered that it was hopeless. The Germans were ever closer to winning.

"Thank God the Americans are in the war with us. They'll be here soon to back us up," an old sergeant told me, as I cleaned his head wound. "That's our only hope."

Soon, Dorothy and I were sharing our hut with two nurses from a hospital nearer the front line. Their hospital had been over-run as the German army advanced. "We all had to clear out in a hurry," the new girls said. "Either that, or be taken prisoner."

There were only two beds, so we had to take turns sleeping, between shifts.

Nurses, doctors, patients, ambulances, stores of bandages, disinfectant and instruments – everything from their hospital had been loaded and moved with them, and now it all had to be put somewhere. The wards were crammed. Patients were sent back to England before they were really fit to travel, just to make space.

"I shouldn't worry," a sour-faced corporal said. "The Germans'll be here any day. Let *them* take over."

I'd never expected to be in the front line! Day by day, the German army came nearer as they made for the coast. Then the hospital itself came under fire.

At first I couldn't believe it when I heard aircraft overhead. *German* aircraft. Then there was the whine and crump of shells, a sickening crash, and a blast of air – close, very close.

For the patients who were already shell-shocked, it was too much to bear. Some of them cowered and whimpered like babies, while others scrambled up in panic and tried to run out of the tent. I was terrified too, but had to get them back to their beds. One desperate man shoved me aside and sent me sprawling. The sound of the aircraft had moved off, but now it was coming back. There was nowhere to

hide, nowhere to shelter. With the next blast I pressed my hands to my ears as the tremor rippled through me. Then I opened my eyes, amazed that I was still alive.

When the planes had gone, the smell of explosive hung in the air.

Three patients and two nurses in the next ward had been killed. Their bodies were laid on stretchers, covered over and put aside.

We carried on clearing up.

That day, I was certain that nothing could stop the Germans from winning.

But the tide was turning. As the days went by, more and more American soldiers arrived in France. They were as fresh and keen as the British troops had been at the beginning. And people said that the Germans were tired of war. They were running out of soldiers. Some of the German prisoners were boys of 15 or 16, who sobbed in pain and fear.

Rumours were flying that the Germans would ask for peace.

I had worked all night and I was asleep in the tent when Dorothy came in and shook me awake.

"The war's over!"

"What?" At first I was only annoyed at being disturbed. "*What?*"

"The war's over. Listen!"

I propped myself up. There was no sound of guns, near or distant. Instead I heard the joyful sound of church bells from the town.

Chapter 10

A Promise Kept

For months now – years – everyone had talked about *after the war*, as if life might be normal again. Now, it didn't feel like that at all. There *was* no normal life.

I stayed on in the hospital for several more weeks. A dreadful flu epidemic kept the wards full. Somehow, I managed not to catch it.

Dorothy and I talked about what we'd do next. Dorothy thought she'd train as a proper nurse, in a London hospital. "What about you?" she asked.

"I don't know. I've had enough of nursing. Father will want me to work in the shop again, but I don't want to stay in the village. Girls do all sorts of work nowadays, don't they? Maybe I'll learn to drive and find work that way."

I still had Harry's photograph, and Georgie's, but I'd put them away in my case. It hurt too much to look at them, for different reasons.

I got home in time for the special church service for all those in the village who had died or were still missing. There were so many faces that weren't there – so many families without their sons, fathers, uncles or brothers. Yet the church was full. Everyone had come.

The vicar talked of plans for a proper memorial. It would stand in the churchyard and would be carved with the names of all the dead. Meanwhile, he read out the list.

"George Peacock, aged 19."

I closed my eyes and thought of Georgie the way I wanted to remember him, whistling and happy, going off to see Bramble the pony.

Now he was lying in a graveyard somewhere in France.

It was all wrong. He should be here, in the churchyard bright with primroses and violets and the promise of spring. He should never have gone to fight in a war he didn't understand.

I didn't realise Harry was there until I left the church.

He was in uniform, standing with his parents, looking at the flowers that had been laid on the grass around a Union Jack flag.

I caught his eye. He looked at me uncertainly.

For a moment I thought I might simply smile and walk past. But I couldn't do that. I had to know.

My parents stopped to speak to Harry's, and here was my chance.

"I waited and waited for your letters, but they never came," I said.

"No."

Our parents had walked on, leaving us.

I had to swallow hard. "Why didn't you –?"

"Tilly," he said in a low voice. "I let you down. I broke my promise. How could you ever forgive me? How could I ask you to?"

"About Georgie?" I asked. "I guessed there was more than you told my parents."

Harry seemed about to speak, but then he shook his head. "Are you going to the village hall?"

We followed the crowd along the lane. I thought of Karl and my own broken promise, and what Sister had told me.

"Harry – what you said. There's nothing to forgive. Really there isn't."

"But there is. I promised to look after Georgie. And – he died."

We were walking slowly, overtaken by others. Instead of going into the hall, we stood together outside.

"But you tried," I said. "I know you did."

"Yes." He looked at me. "But Tilly, when I wrote to your parents, it wasn't the whole truth."

"What wasn't?"

"When – I told you he was happy. At first he was. He liked the routines. He wasn't in my platoon but I tried to make sure he had easy jobs to do – carrying duckboards, that sort of

thing, or sometimes helping with the horses. He loved the horses – well, you know that. But –" He stopped and shook his head.

"Go on," I said softly.

"It was awful, the horses. I know it was awful for the men too – but it seems all wrong to drag horses into a war. Georgie couldn't bear it when he saw dead horses, wounded horses. And even worse ... One day, when we were marching up to the front, we saw a wagon stuck in deep mud. The two horses had been untied, but they were too deep in the mud for anyone to get them out. They were terrified, weak with struggling, their eyes were rolling ... and ..."

"What happened?"

"An officer shot them in front of us. It was the only thing to do."

"Poor horses," I whispered. "Poor Georgie, to see that."

"He couldn't stand it. Just couldn't stand it. He kept weeping, and calling out for Bramble, wanting to find him and look after him. I told him Bramble was safe at home. That night we reached the front line and I was sent to check our wire with two others. I told Georgie to wait in our dugout and make tea for when we got back. I thought it might keep him calm, if he had something to do."

"Oh, Harry. That was a kind thought."

Harry shook his head. "But it didn't save him. The three of us went out and we'd nearly finished when there was a burst of shelling and we had to take cover. Then I heard a shot close by. It was – they'd got Georgie. He'd come out into the open, to look for me, I think, or perhaps to look for Bramble again. A sniper got him. He was shot in the head, Tilly. Killed instantly. That part was true."

I nodded. My eyes blurred as I thought of poor confused Georgie and the horror of what he'd seen.

"And Tilly," Harry said, "he'd made the tea, like I told him. It was there in the dugout, waiting."

"Aren't you two coming in?" the vicar's wife called from the door.

I touched Harry's sleeve. "Thank you. I'm glad you told me."

In the hall there was tea and scones and chat. I drank tea and spoke politely to people. In my mind I was in the scene Harry had described. I was with Georgie, thinking of his distress, his confusion. And I knew what I should have known before – that I hadn't been fair to Harry, getting a promise out of him that he couldn't hope to keep.

I told my parents only part of what Harry had said – about Georgie making the tea. I said nothing about the horses, or Georgie's distress. I wanted them to know that Georgie had tried, had done what he was told right up to the end, and that Harry had been kind to him.

Harry was leaving again soon, to join his unit in Southampton. The war had ended but there was still work to be done, packing up stores, and repairs. Harry wouldn't get his release papers for another month or so. But the war was over and there would never be another. It was the war to end all wars, people said.

Next afternoon Harry called for me. We walked into the churchyard and stood by the wall looking across the fields, where we talked that evening long ago at the start of the war. The trees would soon come into leaf and swallows would nest under the eaves. Some things would be as they'd always been.

There was something important I had to say.

"Harry, I know you've been feeling awful. Guilty. But it's my fault, not yours. You *did* keep your promise, as well as anyone could have. You did look after Georgie. It wasn't your fault he died."

Harry's eyes were full of tears.

"I'm just glad you've come back," I whispered, "when so many haven't."

"Thank you, Tilly."

"And – there was my promise, too," I reminded him. "I promised to wait. Well, I have. Here I am. Here we are."

We were soon parted again. Harry went to Chelmsford, to the station, and I went with him.

I stood on the platform and he opened the carriage window to lean out.

"I'll write," he said. "Promise you'll write back?"

"Every day. I promise."

We could make promises now and be sure of keeping them.

"I love you, Tilly Peacock."

"And I love you, Harry Brading."

The guard blew his whistle. Harry kissed my hand and held it tight. As the train began to pull out I walked beside it on the platform, until we had to let go of each other.

At least, this time, I could be sure he'd come back. And soon.

More **Historical Romance**...

Wild Song

Jane Eagland

Anna's lived on the island all her life.

She knows no one else apart from her father, her father's assistant and two faithful servants.

But one day, a strange boy is washed up on the shore. He's wild and free. And he has the power to change everything...

Timepiece Series

Anne Perry

Troubled school girl Rosie Sands finds a series of very special watches which take her back in time. Rosie finds herself face-to-face with some of the most important women in history as they face their own darkest hours.

Will Rosie be inspired by their courage, or will the dangers of the past engulf her?

Soul Mates

L.A. Weatherly

Why do I keep dreaming about this boy? He's been haunting me for years.

Iris has always felt drawn to Los Angeles. When at last she gets there, she finds herself in front of an old house with a broken iron gate. Inside the house she meets Nate. He's the boy who has haunted her dreams – and she has haunted his.

They are soul mates.

But by meeting, Iris and Nate have placed themselves in great danger. Are they going to be torn apart, just as they have found each other?

A Lily, A Rose

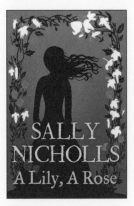

Sally Nicholls

There's not much company for a young lady in Elinor's father's castle. So when Dan comes to the castle to train as a knight, Elinor is delighted. And it's not long before they fall in love.

But Elinor's father has plans for her. Plans that involve a marriage. To one of her father's oldest friends ...

Can Elinor and Dan's love survive?

www.barringtonstoke.co.uk